Some Birds

Matt Spink

David Fickling Books

Some birds are **big**,

some birds are small

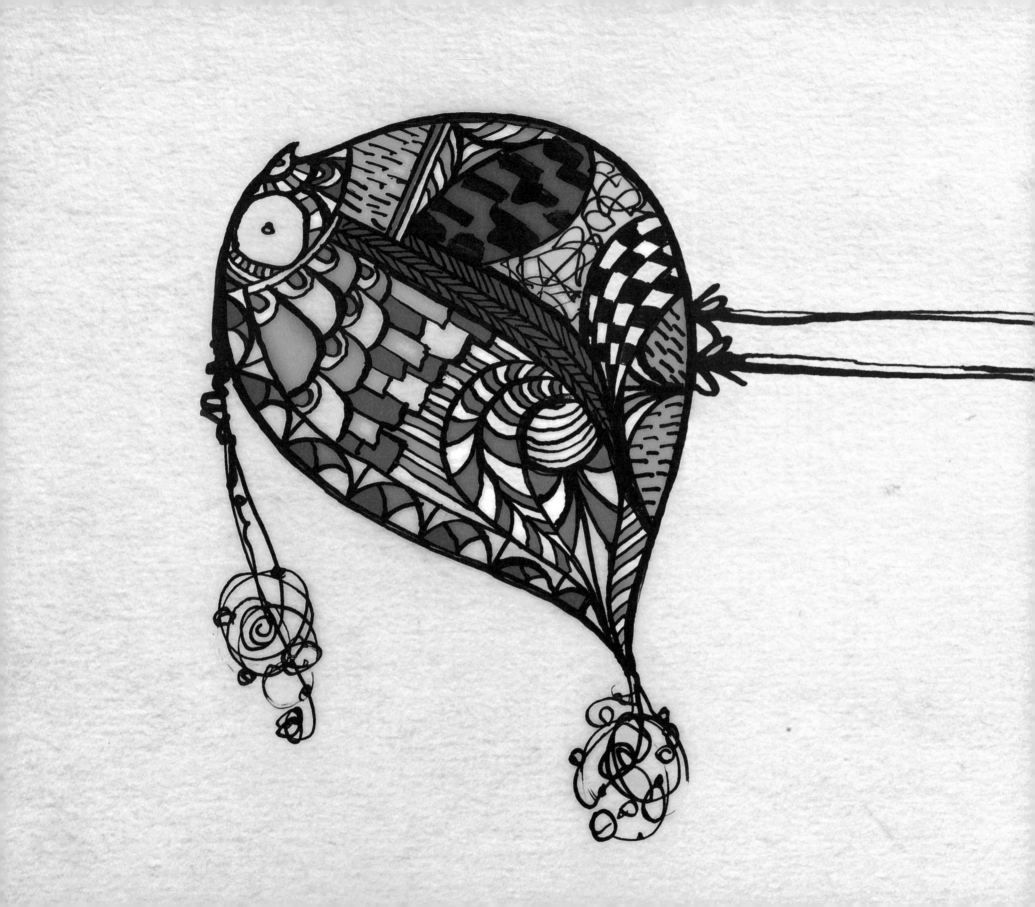

and some birds are just incredibly tall.

Some birds swoop

and some birds **squawk,**

some birds **soar high,**

while some birds just **walk.**

Some birds Waddle.

and some birds eat worms

until they go pop!

Some birds twitch,

some
birds
tweet

and some birds swim fast with

Webbed flipper feet.

Some birds flutter,

some birds

flap

and some birds fly off

to other parts of the map.

Some birds build nests away from sly cats

and some birds make holes with a

rat-a-tat-tat!

Some birds are caged,

but most birds are

I'm sure you'll agree.

To Maddy, Izzy, Lottie
and all the children in the world.

SOME BIRDS
is a
DAVID FICKLING BOOK

First published in Great Britain in 2016
by David Fickling Books, 31 Beaumont Street,
Oxford, OX1 2NP

www.davidficklingbooks.com

Hardback edition published 2016
This edition published 2017

Copyright © Matt Spink

978-1-910200-93-3

Warning: this book will make you FLUTTER, FLAP AND SOAR!

1 3 5 7 9 10 8 6 4 2

DAVID FICKLING BOOKS Reg. No. 8340307

A CIP catalogue record for this book is available from the British Library.

Printed and bound in China

Papers used by David Fickling Books are from responsible sources.

MIX
Paper from
responsible sources
FSC
www.fsc.org   FSC® C104723